MUG PUNTER

Three Capers

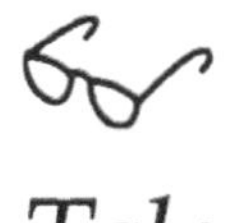

Tale

This is a work of fiction. Names, characters and events are the products of the author's imagination. Any resemblance to actual persons, living or dead, or actual events is purely coincidental.

First Published 2018

National Library of Australia Cataloguing-in-Publication entry:
Creator: New, Robert, author.
Title: Mug Punter: Three Capers.
ISBN: 978-0-6483273-4-9 (paperback)
Subjects: Crime short stories.

Tale Publishing
Melbourne Victoria

Contents

The Coat Hanger

'Art theft, of course,' said the elegant man, 'has been overdone. By now it's thoroughly boring.'[1]

'That's not an answer. Let me confirm I have this right,' Jimmy "Mug" Punter said to his new acquaintance, Bucky Fuller. 'You want me to break into a dry cleaner to steal an item of clothing.'

Mug was in his usual booth in Bacchus Bar at the unusual time of midday. Bucky had appeared by appointment a short while after he'd arrived. The chair at the top end of the booth was too small for Bucky's size. He shifted uncomfortably and glared at Mug like he was a child.

'Yes,' said Bucky, taking a breath and letting his weight drive the air from his lungs. Mug was uncertain his response wasn't just a sonically blessed wheeze.

Mug raised an eyebrow. 'One item?'

'Yes,' Bucky wheezed again.

'What piece of clothing could be worth you paying me forty

---

[1]First line from 'Ask a Silly Question', *Thieves Dozen*, Donald E Westlake

thousand to steal for you?'

'Don't want the clothing, just the coat hanger.'

Mug rolled his eyes.

'Just the coat hanger? Look, far be it for me to refuse a payday, but I'm happy to get you a coat hanger for much less than that. It would be real nice too—wood inlay and gold hook and stuff.'

Bucky sighed. 'You mean *really* nice.'

'Whatever. What's so special about this coat hanger?'

'It contains the key to the secret of success. Look, just get it. You can keep what's on it.'

Mug shook his head. 'It's your money.'

'Time's important. Can you do it tonight?'

'No. There's no way I can plan and execute an operation that quickly.'

'I'll give you an extra five thousand.'

'No.' Mug's voice wavered. 'It can't be done.' He really shouldn't let himself be tempted.

'Extra ten or I'll get someone else.'

'Okay, I'll do it,' Mug said. 'What was the item number again?'

'Two, seven, three, one.' Mug dutifully wrote the number down.

'I muddle numbers sometimes. Can you confirm I've written this correctly?'

Bucky nodded, reached into his jacket pocket and passed over a crumpled business card. 'This is the address.'

'Okay, okay. I've got it,' said Mug.

~

Mug assembled his crew; Slavish was his gadget and safe-cracking guy and Murky was his driver and lookout. An hour later, they were with him at Bacchus Bar.

'Guys, we have a job,' Mug said.

'Oh yeah?' said Murky.

'Yeah, some guy wants us to break into a dry cleaner and steal a coat hanger.' He tried to remain deadpan, but a smile still escaped onto his face.

'What?' Murky and Slavish said in unison.

'Yep. Fifty grand between us to steal a coat hanger.'

'Awesome,' said Murky.

'No way. Why on earth?' said Slavish. 'Wait. Are you having a lend?'

'Nope. Fifty thousand to steal a coat hanger.' Mug smiled. Their reaction had been perfect.

'The best bit is they're a *dry cleaner*. I mean who steals from a dry cleaner? So pretty simple security.'

'Awesome,' said Murky again.

'What's the catch?' asked Slavish.

'Who says there's a catch?' said Mug.

'C'mon Mug, for someone to pay that much for so little, there must be a catch.'

'Well, umm... the job has to be done tonight.'

Slavish stood and reached to shake Mug's hand. 'Thanks for the drink Mug. See you on Saturday.'

'Sit down Slavish. It's not impossible.'

'But it sounds like a setup.'

'It's not. The guy passed the usual checks.'

'Yeah, but what's the rush.'

'He wants to get it before someone else collects the item tomorrow.'

'I'll humour you. What are the details?'

'The dry cleaner is on Oxford Street and we're after item...' Mug checked his bit of paper, 'two, seven, three, one.'

'Mmmm.' Slavish nodded. 'What else?'

Mug shrugged. 'That's all I know.'

'No details on security, no entry or exit plan and no means of concealing the item if we get caught.'

'Yep,' said Mug.

'No plan then, just wing it?' said Slavish.

'It worked for us on that job Murky brought us last year.'

'Which you hated,' Murky said. 'You were pissed we had to abandon your plan.'

'Yeah, well maybe I learnt we could do things more simply.'

'Or you just want the money,' Murky suggested.

Mug smiled. 'Maybe. It's a simple job though, and no need to fence anything.'

'True. A simple payday could be good. I'm in,' said Slavish.

'Me too,' said Murky.

~

The dry cleaner was in the middle of a long row of shops. It had a carpark at the back, where Mug, Murky and Slavish were huddled in Murky's nondescript brown van. Murky had placed a sign on the sides of the van reading "James's Drycleaning," the name of the business they were about to break into. It wasn't a good sign as it was just painted on a magnetic whiteboard, but they all agreed it was better than nothing.

'How long do you want to be in there for?' asked Murky.

'No more than sixty seconds. We should just be in and out. I mean all we have to do is go in, find one item and leave.'

'No way you'll be in and out in that time,' said Murky.

'Oh yeah, wanna bet?' asked Mug.

'What's my share?'

'Just under seventeen thousand,' replied Mug.

'Three thousand says you won't be outside in ninety.'

'You're on.'

'I'll take a hundred secs,' said Slavish.

'What are we saying?' asked Murky.

'Let's make it fifteen grand each and bonus five to the person whose time is closest,' suggested Mug.

'Done,' the others replied in unison.

'Starting from when the shop door is open to when you've got the item and have left the building,' said Murky.

'Of course.' Mug looked at Slavish. 'And no going slow just to win.'

'Thieves' honour.' Slavish grinned, 'Who's timing?'

'Me,' said Murky. 'I'll keep you informed over coms.'

Mug and Slavish put on their hoodies and fake glasses and got out of the van. They grinned when they saw the door had electronic locks. Slavish found the external fuse box, picked the padlock on it and quickly shut the power to the block of shops. A few metres away they could see the dry cleaner's door release and open a couple of centimetres.

~

Mug and Slavish entered the dry cleaners. Along the side wall was a narrow bench with a sewing machine. The rest of the store was filled by a suspended, mechanised track which twisted and turned so it occupied most of the space. Hanging from the track's rack were what looked like a thousand items of clothing inside plastic bags. Mug and Slavish glanced at each other and shrugged. There was no order to the numbers on the tags. The track was designed to bring the required item to the front when it's number was typed into a keypad by the front counter. The tags were scanned as they passed the collection point.

'Twenty seconds,' said Murky into their ears.

They soon found where to turn the track on, but then realised that by cutting the power it wouldn't work.

'I didn't bring the gear to power this ourselves. It would take too long to set up anyway. Plus, they'd know we'd been here if the rack moved,' said Slavish.

'Fine. We'll just have to look for it ourselves.' They began scanning the tags.

'What was the number again?'

'Two, seven, three, one.'

'Nope, this was two, one, three, seven.'

'Forty seconds,' said Murky. Mug and Slavish tried to speed up their searching.

'This is ridiculous. It's almost the proverbial needle,' said Slavish.

'Yep.'

'One minute,' said Murky, his voice rising in excitement.

'Dammit. I'm out,' said Mug unhappily.

'Seventy seconds,' said Murky.

Mug kept reading the numbers. 'Got it,' he said as he grabbed an item and raced for the exit.

'Eighty-nine seconds. Looks like I win!' Murky said, unable to keep the grin out of his voice. Mug and Slavish scowled. In the back of the van, they looked at the dress on the coat hanger.

'Slavish, you can have the dress for your girl. Looks like it would suit her,' Murky said with false magnanimity.

The dress was bright red and cut to be revealing. Slavish's frown turned briefly to a smile. He was probably picturing his girlfriend in the dress.

Fifteen minutes later, they were back in Bacchus Bar and had ordered a round of celebratory drinks. Mug phoned Bucky to say they had the item he was after and were in the bar waiting for him.

~

Bucky blocked the light from the doorway as he entered. He

walked with some effort over to the bar and spoke briefly to the Rick the bartender, before joining them at the booth. He placed a briefcase on the table.

'Where is it?'

Mug handed over the coat hanger, with the item tag still attached.

Bucky turned red. 'Is this a joke?'

'What do you mean?'

'I wanted item two, seven, three, one, not one, three.' Bucky looked like he was about to explode. He put his hand on his heart as though he was having a heart attack.

'Dammit Mug, you know you're meant to check with us when your dyslexia could be an issue,' said Slavish.

'There wasn't time,' Mug said apologetically. Thanks to the damn bet.

'I'm sorry for the mistake. If you don't mind waiting, I know it's nearly midnight, but the bar doesn't close until two. We'll be back within thirty minutes,' Mug said as politely as he could. He looked guiltily at Slavish and Murky.

Bucky signalled to Rick to cancel his order as the others ran from the bar.

~

Mug and Slavish approached the back door of the dry cleaner. In their rush, they hadn't noticed a policeman in the shadows who emerged and approached them.

'Hello Gents. There was a report of some unusual activity earlier this evening. I'm afraid you'll have to come back tomorrow.'

Over the in-ear coms, Mug heard the sound of Murky getting out of the car to remove the magnetic signs on the van.

'But they advertise twenty-four-hour pick up,' Slavish moaned.

Mug just managed to stifle a laugh.

'The door's open, but it seems like the power is off. I'll get it for you. What's the number?'

'Two, seven, three, one,' they said in unison.

'Okay. You wait here.'

A minute later the policeman returned and handed a dry-cleaning bag to Mug. Mug took it and hoped he concealed his disbelief by saying, 'Thank you.'

They walked as normally as they could manage to the van, grateful they'd parked around the corner from the store. All three double-checked the number. Only then did Mug and Slavish burst out laughing.

Slavish continued to grin after the others stopped.

'What's up with you?' asked Mug.

'Don't you see I won,' he said triumphantly.

'Won what?'

'The bet. It took well over 100 seconds to retrieve the item, so I win.'

'Nup,' said Murky, 'I won fair and square.'

They both looked to Mug.

'The bet was how long it would take to get the coat hanger and get out. You added that bit Murky.'

'So?'

'We didn't get the right one until now. And that's about a few thousand seconds. One hundred is nearest to that.'

Murky appeared crestfallen. 'Dammit.'

Mug laughed, while Slavish grinned even more broadly.

'Don't worry Murky, this time you can keep the clothing.' They all looked at the dark blue suit. It would probably suit Murky. Maybe he'd wear it to his court appearance in a few weeks.

~

As they re-entered Bacchus Bar, Bucky signalled to Rick, who nodded in response. The group sat in their booth. Mug was surprised Bucky hadn't tried to take their seats, but then he realised Bucky wouldn't fit in the booth. The briefcase was still on the table. Mug gave him the coat hanger.

Bucky smiled and started unwinding the coat hanger with a pair of pliers he'd produced from his jacket pocket. Rick brought over a large bowl of steaming water he held with oven mitts, and then fetched a glass of cold water.

Mug and Murky looked confused. Slavish smiled. 'Oh wow,' he said.

'What?' asked Mug and Murky in unison.

'Is the wire nitinol?' asked Slavish, his eyes widening.

'Yes, how'd you know about that?' asked Bucky, without looking up from trying to untangle the wire.

'I did most of a mech eng degree a few years ago.'

'Mmm,' Bucky's replied was barely a grunt, nevertheless the surprise showed on his face.

Slavish spoke enthusiastically. 'Nitinol is what they call a shape memory alloy. It's a special blend of metals that has a crude form of memory. Basically you form it into a shape at high temperature, cool it and then you can make it into any shape you want. When you heat it again it'll return to the shape you set at the high temperature.'

'Wait. You're trying to tell me a piece of metal can have a memory,' asked Mug.

'Yes.'

'You're nuts,' said Murky.

'Not according to my doctor,' Slavish said with a grin. 'Just watch.'

Bucky finished unravelling the coat hanger. He lowered it into the bowl of near boiling water. Murky and Mug gasped as the metal began twisting by itself. It transformed until it had formed a new shape which looked like a series of numbers.

'Cool isn't it?' said Slavish. 'You know, I've never thought of using it to conceal a code, but it's actually a pretty awesome idea. I mean you could make it into anything and no one would know you were hiding something. It could be the spring in a ballpoint pen, the underwire on a bra, part of a suitcase…' Slavish trailed off as he started thinking of the possibilities.

'Thank you,' Bucky wheezed as he handed over a bulging envelope. 'It's got uses. Now stop talking and let me…'

The group fell silent as Bucky entered the code into the electronically controlled briefcase. It gave a satisfying click as it unlocked. Bucky opened the case to reveal a bottle of Scotch and a sheet of paper.

'This, gentlemen, is one of the finest whiskies in the world, but it's not the most valuable thing here. On that sheet of paper is the secret of success. I had someone else steal the case for me yesterday. Their owner will have discovered this by now and will suspect me as I recently drafted his will and made a lot of comments about wanting to know what was written on here.'

Bucky pointed to the paper. 'I couldn't believe he was going to leave it to his son, who would probably mix the whisky with cola, and not appreciate the wisdom.'

Bucky shuddered, his huge frame taking a while to settle again. He reached for his heart once more and then took a sip of water.

He picked up the piece of paper and began reading silently.

~

The secret of success comes from accepting a facet of human nature; the average person feels losses twice as much as gains. This leads to a loss aversion— a hesitancy to accept risk even when the odds are in your favour. Most people, when confronted with a fifty-fifty bet would baulk at wagering if they were risking as much as they could gain. So, if offered a chance to win or lose ten dollars on the result of a coin toss, the average person would say no or might try once and then stop due to the fear of losing money. Regardless, the smart man wouldn't take this bet repeatedly. However, if you altered the odds so they were in your favour such as you only risking $4 to win $6 on a coin toss, then over repeated trials you'd make a significant amount of money. However, due to loss aversion, many still wouldn't take this bet as they're too afraid of losing. The trick to turning this understanding into long-term success is to realise it's not about gambling at all. It's about not viewing each opportunity in your life as a unique event. It's about understanding how life is a series of little moments, little chances where accepting a moderate amount of risk could lead to reward. Sure, you'll lose some of the time, but over multiple opportunities, on aggregate, you'll come out ahead. So publish that story, invest in that start-up, tell that person how you really feel. Take *all* the opportunities you can which are slightly more likely to work out, than not. That is the secret of success.

~

Bucky smiled and put the paper into his pocket without saying what was on it. 'I have to say hiding the code for the briefcase was ingenious, but a smart person wouldn't have revealed all the details in a single document, even if it was their will.'

Bucky continued to talk as he closed the briefcase, his voice no longer directed at anyone in particular.

'I'll most likely be dead tomorrow, either because my client has killed me or my heart has given out—the doctor has given me two weeks. Once I've passed that paper on to my son, I'll crack the whisky and I can die a happy man. Goodbye gentlemen.'

Bucky stood and walked unsteadily out of the bar, taking the briefcase with him. In a state of shock, Mug silently divided the money from the envelope. He looked at the twisted coat hanger on the table and sighed. Murky and Slavish nodded.

'Thanks Mug that's one for the grandkids,' said Murky.

'Here, you may as well have this too,' said Mug as he handed the wire to Slavish.

'Thirty grand, a magic wire, a dress for my girl, and a tale to tell,' Slavish said. 'Best night in ages!'

The Argument

Jimmy 'Mug' Punter and his recently acquired friend Dr Engels were sitting in Mug's customary booth at the back of Bacchus Bar. Mug was nursing a single malt, as was his friend. They were musing over Mug's role in the Dr Engels' ongoing attempt to socially engineer a political party which would unite people and bring about wholesale social change.

'You know there's a fatal flaw in your plan don't you?' Mug asked.

'What?' Dr Engels inquired. Mug was amazed someone of Dr Engels stature seemed interested in his point of view.

'Greed. I mean people want to have more or be more than others. It's human nature.'

'Is it?'

'Yes.'

They both settled into silence and sipped their whiskies appreciatively.

'What do we do about that?' Dr Engels asked.

'What do you mean 'we'?'

'Come now, you know you're involved in this project, one way or another.'

'Yeah, but I've done my bit; I stole you the manifesto.'

'You did, and what a manifesto it is,' Dr Engels said as he raised his glass to Mug's. They clinked and took another sip. Dr Engels signalled to Rick the bartender to bring them another round. As Rick brought the drinks over, a couple entered the bar, bringing with them an air of hostility.

'I mean,' said Mug, 'take a look at those two. They're clearly arguing about something.'

Dr Engels turned and looked. The couple was far enough away that the din of the bar made their words unintelligible. However, their glaring eyes and body language said they were very angry at each other.

'Yes.' Dr Engels nodded.

'That's why you won't reach everyone. Clearly they each want something different to the other.'

'I know why they're arguing,' Dr Engels replied softly.

'Wait, what?' Mug said.

'I know why they're arguing,' Dr Engels repeated more confidently.

'How? I mean, I happen to know them well enough to know what they're probably fighting about. But how could you know? There's no way.'

'Of course I can. There's only one reason why people argue that passionately,' Dr Engels said with a mischievous smirk.

'Which is?' asked Mug.

'Now now, don't spoil the game.' Dr Engels smiled.

'What game?'

'Let's make a wager. It's how you earnt your nickname isn't it?'

'Maybe. What's the bet?' Mug leant forward.

'If I can tell what they're arguing about you buy the next

round.'

Mug waved his hand. 'Pfft. That's not a wager,' he said.

'Okay then, how about whatever's left in a bottle from the top shelf?' said Dr Engels.

Mug thought that was more like it.

'You know Rick has a thirty-year-old malt up there?'

Dr Engels pointed to his glass.

'Who do you think he keeps it there for?'

'Alrighty then. I think we have our stakes sorted. What are the terms?'

'I'll write down what I think the reason is. You get Rick to take it to them and tell them if what I've written is true, they should nod to us. If not, then shake their heads.'

'Okay,' said Mug.

'Nodding means I get what's left of the bottle, a shake means you do.'

'Yeah, that's what we said. Geez, you're a stickler for details.'

'You knew that already.'

'Yeah, I guess I did,' said Mug.

Dr Engels signalled to Rick to come over to them. While they were waiting, Dr Engels took a pen from his pocket and wrote what appeared to be a short sentence or two on a napkin.

'Done,' he said to Mug.

'Really? Didn't seem like much... You'd better not have asked them to nod at us.' Mug frowned.

'I would never do such a thing. It's simply when dealing with such things it's better to say less because there's less for them to disagree with.'

Rick finished serving a customer and came over.

'What can I do for my top shelf customers?' Rick grinned.

'We've got a little wager, we'd like you to help settle,' Mug said.

Rick looked surprised. 'Oh Mug, you do know how you got your nickname don't you?'

'Yeah, but I'm on a winner here,' Mug said confidently.

'And I think he's not, which brings us to the favour we'd like to ask,' said Dr Engels. He explained what they wanted Rick to do and the terms of the wager. Rick smiled at the thought of selling the rest of his most expensive bottle of whisky.

~

Mug watched intensely as Rick walked over to the still arguing couple. They looked even more upset when their argument was interrupted, but seemed to calm down as Rick went through his story and they realised Mug was involved. They gave Mug a wave hello. Rick handed them the napkin. As Rick returned to the bar, they each read it in turn. They turned to the booth and both nodded, looking dumbfounded. Their mood seemed to lift. Whatever Dr Engels had written on the napkin had done more than just identify their disagreement. A couple of minutes later they left arm-in-arm.

'What the hell did you write?' Mug asked, unable to keep the surprise out of his voice.

'Go and see,' Dr Engels said with a twinkle in his eye, 'there's only one reason why people argue. I simply wrote it down.'

Mug stood up while shaking his head. Dr Engels smiled.

'And get Rick to bring the bottle over. I'll pour one for you too.'

Mug walked over to the table and picked up the napkin which had been left on the table. He turned it over and read, 'YOUR TRUTHS ARE NOT THE SAME.'

Just below, seemingly written as an afterthought was: 'BESIDES, IT'S NOT MEANT TO BE THE TWO OF YOU AGAINST EACH OTHER, IT'S MEANT TO BE THE TWO OF YOU VERSUS THE PROBLEM.'

The Second Safe

'Let me get this straight, you want me to break into your *parent's* home and rob a safe,' Jimmy 'Mug' Punter asked his new acquaintance. They were sitting in a booth at the back of Bacchus Bar. A few minutes before, Mug had watched the middle-aged woman, with greying hair and piercing eyes, order two drinks from the bar and look around. When their eyes met she headed straight towards him. She knew who he was. The lady had introduced herself as Justine Time and handed him a Single Malt. She knew his drink too. Mug had frowned as she sat down without an invitation.

'No. I want you to break in and rob *two* safes. You may keep the contents of the first, but the second, you bring to me.' The conviction in her voice rang alarm bells. Never do a job when emotion is involved. Mug wondered if he should tell her to leave. But then again, she was not his usual type of client and his curiosity was piqued.

'What's so special about this second safe?'

Justine gave an enigmatic smile.

'I'll try a different question. Why do you want to rob from your parents? Can't you just ask them for whatever it is?'

'What it is, is what I deserve after they gave me this ridiculous name and their continued attempts to control my life. I mean the teasing as a kid plus having to marry someone from the right sort of family, have the right sort of career...'

'It's not a pseudonym? I thought you were being funny.'

'No, but obviously they thought they were,' Justine said bitterly.

'It could be worse, I went to school with a girl named Iona Cox…' Mug said with a grin. Justine winced.

'How do I know this is not a setup?'

'Because I was told to say only the foolhardy would embark on such an adventure to you in response to that question.' Mug nodded acknowledging the code phrase he'd created to help him weed out any narks.

'By who?'

'You mean by whom, and the answer is Murky Thomas.'

'How on earth do you know Murky?'

'I saved his kid's life.'

'Oh, you're *that* doctor.'

'Yes.'

'Wait, that means you're Dr. Time!' Mug said mirthfully. 'That's the coolest name ever.' Mug frowned as he was sure he would've noticed if Murky had said that was his daughter's saviour's name.

Justine scowled in response. 'Ughh. I wasn't going to say it but I got married. My name is Dr Knowles.'

'Shame, Dr Time is much better,' Mug replied making Justine laugh. Mug felt himself relax after recognising the name Murky had told him.

'Now you know who I am, will you do this for me?'

Mug felt like he'd struggle to say no to anything Justine asked him for, even though she was too old for him to be interested in her.

'Why can't I say no to you?'

'You'll have to ask yourself.'

Why can't I say no to her? … She's a damsel in distress and has chosen you to be her knight in shining armour. Mug nodded to himself.

'And because it will please me.' Justine said as though she were reading his thoughts and his Mistress. Mug felt himself liking her more and more.

'Tell me about the safes.'

'The first one is hidden behind our family portrait—'

'Behind a painting. Really? Was the cliché shop having a sale?'

'Probably. Mum never misses one,' Justine replied without missing a beat.

'What's in it?'

'There are two gold ingots, they're a kilo each and worth about fifty thousand apiece, plus some cash and their wills. Leave the wills and take the rest. The safe is a Pandora LS987.'

'Okay,' Mug said slowly as he contemplated the information. He knew the brand had a good reputation. He'd need his friend Slavish in on this one.

'What about the second safe?'

'Like I said, you will see what's in it when you get there, I don't know what model that one is, nor exactly what's in it.'

'Can you at least tell me size and weight?'

'I'm not meant to know the safe exists. I went to the cellar to get a bottle of wine for dinner and when I walked through the cellar door—'

‘Such a beautiful expression – cellar door I mean.’

‘Stop interrupting. Anyway, I never liked the echo when the door shut, so I closed it silently. When I reached the corner of the stairs, I saw Dad standing in front of the wine rack. He twisted three bottles and a section shifted forward. He lifted it up and revealed a safe – the second safe – and I saw him put something in it.’

‘What?’

‘I couldn’t quite see from where I was, but that’s what I want.’

‘You mean you don’t know what you want me to steal?’

Mug shook his head.

‘I know it’s valuable to my parents. I can use it to force them to let me be free to start a new life.’

Mug raised an eyebrow. She must be nearly fifty and she was still under her parent’s thumb. Mug shook his head again.

‘Let’s just say I’m starting the process of divorcing my husband and they’ll put a stop to it when they find out. I want them to let me see it through.’

‘Okay,’ Mug said, ‘how do you know it’s not porn or something similar which your Dad doesn’t want your Mum knowing about?’

‘Because he has a mistress for that, that’s why the cash is in the safe,’ Justine said nonchalantly.

‘And you know that?’

‘We all know that. Look if we spoke about our problems or dealt with them maturely, you and I would not be having this conversation would we?’

‘I guess not. I still think it’s porn though. Maybe we should make a wager?’

‘No.’ Justine was firm in her response. Mug sighed.

‘What’s the security like at the house?’

'It's more of a mansion. There's a two-metre high wall around the property, eight bedrooms… It's got its own ballroom, so you get the idea.'

Mug rolled his eyes.

'There's an automatic gate—'

'Not a concern. You've made it seem like it would be easy enough to carry out the loot, we would probably just jump the wall.'

'We?' Justine questioned, seeming concerned for the first time.

'Listen lady, you might think this is a simple job, but it isn't. The alarms and entry, I can do, but the safes are another matter. My mate Slavish will need to help me with them and then there's the lookout, which will probably be Murky.'

'I was thinking it would be a one-man operation.'

'No it isn't. Which brings me to my next point. Money.'

'You get the money from the safe and the gold like we discussed.'

'Yes, but the gold we will only get about thirty percent of its value at best when we sell it to a fence, which winds up at not much per person given the risk of a few years in jail—'

'You're forgetting the cash.'

'I am?'

'Yes, it's likely to be around fifty thousand.'

'For a mistress?'

'It's also emergency hush money.'

'Why not go public with that then?'

'I'm not trying to humiliate my family, just get away from them.'

Mug nodded and quickly calculated how much each man would earn from the operation. He liked to think of his thefts as operations – he went in with a surgically precise plan and made sure he had contingencies. He would disturb the exterior as little as possible, find what he'd been commissioned to take and remove it like a surgeon removing an appendix.

'You have a deal. Tell me, are there dogs? Other pets? Staff?'

'There's a Jack Russell but they'll take him with them so no, no pets. The staff knock off on Friday at 5pm and won't return until Monday morning. There's a groundskeeper, but he resides in a separate residence on the other side of the property. He keeps to himself and will probably have drunk himself to sleep by the time you get there.'

'When would you like it done?'

'They go away for the week on the twenty-first, it would seem like a good time.'

'Tell me more about the house – layout I mean.'

'I can do one better, here are the floorplans.' Justine reached into her bag and pulled out a folded A3 sheet of paper. Mug smiled. She was a prepared woman. Mug looked at the plans and rapidly formulated a plan.

'The tricky part will be getting out of the house if the alarm goes off. It is designed to trap you inside until the police arrive. Bars come down the windows and the door magnetically locks. Do not set it off,' Justine said emphatically.

'Actually, I intend to,' said Mug with a grin, 'but only as we leave.'

'What? Why on earth would you do that?' Justine said.

'I take it you want us to leave enough evidence of a break-in so suspicion falls away from you? I know you want to blackmail your parents with what we get, but you could cover yourself so it seems like someone sent you the item for some reason. Otherwise, your parents could have you arrested or wind up blackmailing *you.*'

'Good thinking. But you won't be able to escape.'

'Probably not, but that's our problem. Write your phone number on the blueprints for me. I'll be in touch when it's done.' Mug stood up to end the meeting. Justine thanked him and quickly left the bar.

~

Mug took out his phone and called Murky to confirm Justine's story and appearance and see if he wanted in on the operation. Murky said yes, citing ongoing medical costs for his daughter. Next was a quick call to Slavish. Within an hour they were all sitting in the booth at Bacchus Bar together. Murky just seemed to appear next to Mug, as was his way, and Slavish sauntered in with a girl on his arm whom he left at the bar before joining Mug and Murky in their booth.

'Let me get this straight, you *want* us to set off the alarm?' asked Slavish with disbelief.

'Yes,' said Mug as clearly as possible in the noisy bar.

'Why?' Murky practically shouted.

'You'll see,' said Mug with a grin. 'Here's the plan…'

Mug pulled out the blueprints and went through his ideas about how to rob the two safes, how they'd make it seem like Justine had nothing to do with it despite her winding up with some of the loot and how they'd get away with it. When he was finished, Slavish confirmed the type of alarm and the make and models of the safes and how he'd be able to open them.

'Are we all agreed on the plan then?' queried Mug.

'If you're sure being caught won't mean being caught then I guess so,' Slavish said as he glanced at his girlfriend. Mug was sure he was daydreaming about what they could do with the money.

'Uh huh,' grunted Murky managing to agree with Slavish and answer Mug at the same time.

~

Two weeks and a rehearsal at Murky's house later, the trio were ready for the operation. They gathered the tools they'd need and walked around the corner to Murky's non-descript brown van. Murky quickly attached some magnetic signs which said the van belonged to 'Mr. Lead's emergency plumbing services.' The signs had a phone number which would automatically go to voicemail if anyone tried it. Murky had attached some fake licence plates over the van's real ones. They knew if someone took a close look at the van they might spot they were fakes, but they also knew they were going to a very quiet neighbourhood, with decent spacing between houses. It was unlikely anyone would see them at all, let alone get close enough to notice the signage was an add-on.

Justine's parent's home was daunting. It was on two acres of land in the wealthiest suburb of the city. According to the floorplans besides the eight bedrooms and ballroom there was not one, but two libraries. 'Why two?' Mug had asked Justine sarcastically. 'One for fiction, one for non-fiction, each requires a different setting to be appreciated properly,' she'd replied deadpan. Mug had laughed and rolled his eyes.

The trio exited the van and pulled Slavish's specially designed ladder from the roof. Slavish had all but finished a degree in mechanical engineering when he'd been nabbed for the first time. By the time he got out of prison, he'd spent so much time daydreaming about devices to make crime easier, it just seemed unnecessary to complete the degree or get a real job. The ladder was a work of mechanical ingenuity and did not have the traditional cross-bar arm of an A-frame. Instead, there was a clamp which could attach to a surface up to three bricks wide. Attached to the bottom step was a rope so once they'd climbed over the double brick wall, all they had to do was pull on the rope to lift the ladder over them. The runners Slavish had designed were near silent and made it a breeze to use and enabled the ladder to simply flip over the fence and out of sight of the street.

'T'is a thing of genius, Slavish,' Mug said softly, when they were safely over the fence and standing on the lush green lawn on the other side. They easily unhooked the ladder and lay it down, ready to use when they needed to leave.

'Thanks Mug,' Slavish whispered back. Mug started looking for anything that might interfere with their carefully formulated plan.

'There's a dog,' Mug whispered with urgency.

'What's it doing here?' Murky asked from over the fence.

'Checking its wee-mail,' Mug shot back.

'Shit,' said Murky louder than he meant to.

'No that's not what I … wait… actually yeah that's what it's doing now.'

Slavish nudged Mug. 'Do we call it off?'

'No it has to be today. This is the only time they're away,' replied Mug.

'You sure it was this weekend they were away and they were leaving on a Friday? You know you get things back to front sometimes,' Slavish said.

'Leave my *lysdexia* out of this. She definitely said they were going away for the weekend on the twelfth.'

'Are you sure? Maybe it was the twenty-first?'

'I'd considered that 'cos I thought I'd heard the twenty-first, but that would make it a Sunday – who goes away for the weekend on a Sunday?' Mug asked rhetorically.

'Fair enough, but they're here.'

'Can you come back on the twenty-first?' Mug hissed.

'No, that's the big game. There's no way I'm missing it.'

'And you Murky?' asked Mug over the fence.

'It's Annie's school play. Given everything this year, I'd say it's definitely a no-can-miss.'

'The house is huge, maybe we just sneak in now. They're probably in bed by now anyway. Plus the alarm would be off,' Slavish suggested.

'What about the plan?' Mug didn't want to see the plan wasted.

'Scrap it, let's switch to plan C,' Slavish said.

'Leg it and regroup at Bacchus?'

'Fine Plan D then.'

'There is no plan D,' Mug hissed.

'Exactly, let's just wing it.'

Mug couldn't believe they were going to go in with no plan.

'Murky you got that? The plan is to go to jail,' he said over the fence.

'What?' Murky replied as loudly as he dared.

'Nevermind. We're going in without a plan,' Mug responded with mock enthusiasm.

'Oh okay. I'll keep my hand on the ignition then.' Murky replied.

'What are we going to do?' asked Slavish.

'Stick with the original plan, minus the whole setting off the alarm thing,' replied Mug as they activated his in-ear coms.

Mug and Slavish worked in unison to adjust the ladder to its alternate configuration – a conventional extension ladder, which they used to access the roof at their chosen point. Slavish then set about removing roof tiles, while Mug lassoed the nearby chimney and dropped some coils of rope into the hole Slavish had created. Once inside the roof cavity they located the manhole which would give them access to the floor of the home.

One after the other, they dropped silently onto the floor of one of the five bathrooms in the home, leaving the rope dangling to let them reach the high ceiling on the way out.

'Which one first?'

'The one behind the painting. Payment first, prize second.'

'Yep.'

They walked silently, their *jika-tabi* boots were flexible and gave them a tactile sense of contact with the ground. Mug loved the boots as they made him feel like a ninja even though he'd never set foot inside a *dojo*. Each had a backpack containing the tools they would need. Mug shone the torch in front of them as they walked.

When they reached the dining room, they moved to the doors at either end and pulled out several wooden wedges to slide underneath the doors. The wedges were part of their standard practice. Their purpose was twofold, to give them time if anyone came to stop them and to block the light they would need while they worked. Slavish flicked on the light switch. Mug stifled a laugh. The painting, which Justine had described as a family portrait, was hideously ostentatious. It showed Justine seated in a chair and her parents either side of her. Each had one possessive hand on her shoulder, knuckles clearly showing. The spacing between each of them and their expressions indicated a family which wasn't particularly fond of each other.

'Tells a story doesn't it?' Mug said whimsically.

'Yep,' Slavish replied.

'Let's do what we gotta do.'

In silence they felt around the edge of the painting, until Slavish found the latch to release the painting to swing on its hidden hinge.

The safe was exactly as Justine had described and Slavish grinned as he set to work opening it. This was his favourite part of the job. The safe was tricky to crack, but like most safes, Slavish had realised, its vulnerability lay in the strengths it had been designed for, not the weaknesses it carried. Any attempt to remove the entire safe would be problematic as it was impossible to know how well anchored it was within the wall. The door was the entire front face of the safe and the hinges were hidden inside. Slavish had ruled out drilling into the safe and plopping in some explosives as it would destroy the money and the documents within, and the lack of electronics meant the safe could not be hacked. The tumblers operated silently so using a stethoscope wouldn't work. The only way in was turning the three tumblers in the right order, to their right numbers. Slavish was up for the challenge. He could tell from the painting and his colleagues' descriptions of Justine that doing things the right way was important to the family, which mean the correct sequence would be from left to right. Slavish removed the gloves from his hands. If they were interrupted, he would be leaving fingerprints, but this part of the job required the utmost sensitivity from his fingertips.

Slavish pulled out his earpiece and put in earplugs. Mug watched him close his eyes to reduce the sensory load on his brain and accentuate the information from his fingertips. Slavish rested one hand on the safe door and turned the dial with the other. He was slow but consistent. If he stopped at the wrong time the tumbler would need to be reset.

Mug knew, despite years of trying, Slavish had never been able to build a device capable of detecting the tumbler moving into place in this brand of safe, but one night, after falling asleep on top of one and dreaming about opening it, he'd awoken to find the safe open. Ever since, he'd found himself able to *sense* when the tumbler slotted into place. Mug didn't quite believe the story, but he ran with it since it worked.

Two minutes later and Slavish had the safe open.

'I don't know how you do it,' Mug said with admiration.

'You know, I'm not actually sure myself. I don't really believe it's possible to just feel when it's in the right spot.'

'And yet here we are.'

'Yep,' Slavish said with a grin.

They grabbed the gold and cash and wiped the surface of the safe to remove fingerprints.

'Justine was right, there's gotta be at least fifty K here,' Mug said with excitement.

They both grinned. Mug slung his backpack over his shoulder. Slavish did the same.

'Gee this gold is heavy,' said Slavish.

'It's only two kilo's… you really should work out more you know.'

'Look who's talking.'

'Yeah, yeah, let's get on with it.' Mug turned off the lights and used his torch to gather the blocks from the doors.

They made their way to the cellar as quietly as possible. Mug opened the heavy wooden door and let Slavish past. He closed it so softly it barely made a sound. Mug congratulated himself on his mastery of the art of stealth, then froze and put a finger to his lips.

'You remember that quote about the curious incident of the dog in the night?' Mug whispered to Slavish after a pause.

Slavish nodded.

'Well, we don't have that problem.' Mug replied as the sound of a dog snuffling at the door got louder. 'Let's just do what we're here for and hopefully, he'll be gone by the time we get back.'

'Yep,' said Slavish.

Mug took out the wedges and placed them under the door. 'That should stop him smelling us and maybe hearing us for now.'

They moved down the steps as quickly as they could to get

away from the door. Mug stopped at the bottom step to see if he could still hear the dog. He gave Slavish a thumbs up signal and they walked to the back of the cellar.

'Maybe we should nab a few bottles while we're here? They look like they're good drops,' said Slavish.

'No, we only nab what we're being paid to nab,' said Mug, managing to sound principled.

'You know we're criminals, right?'

'Just open it,' Mug replied as the actuator lifted the bottles to reveal the hidden safe.

'Right. We're dealing with another Pandora. But this one's the WS313. It could be a problem.'

'Yes, I see,' said Mug as they both looked at the electronic panel.

'I can't do my spider sense trick on it, but this one I can hack…it will take me probably ten minutes, could you go check on the dog?'

'Sure.'

Mug went to check on the cellar door. The wedges were still in place. He carefully shifted one out and peered underneath the door. There were no signs of the dog or any signs of alarm. Mug breathed a sigh of relief and went back to Slavish.

'Looks ok,' he said to Slavish who had so many wires around him, he seemed to have become part robot.

'Good. I'll be another two minutes.'

One minute and fifty-nine seconds later the safe whirred and the door released. Slavish beamed with pride.

'Shall we see what it is her family want kept extra-secret?' Mug asked.

'Yes,' Slavish replied, clearly curious.

'Hey guys,' said a voice which seemed to come from right next to them. They both jumped. Mug tapped his chest. 'Geez Murk, you gave us a heart attack.'

'Just reminding you I'm here and asking what's taking you so long,' Murky said.

'Long story, we'll tell you later. We'll be another fifteen or so,' Mug replied.

'Sure thing,' Murky replied.

'Now let's get back to the safe,' Mug said to Slavish.

'Yup.'

Mug went to reach for the door. 'Hey it's my turn to open it,' complained Slavish.

'Fine,' Mug replied reluctantly.

Mug was sure Slavish deliberately obscured his view as he opened the door.

'Wow,' Slavish said sounding surprised, 'that's what the big secret is?'

'What is it?' Mug asked. Slavish moved out of the way to let him see.

'Huh?' Mug examined the object then put it in his backpack. Slavish started unclipping wires. A few moments later, they were ready to leave.

Mug retrieved the wedges and silently closed the cellar door. Together they made their way to the bathroom. It seemed undisturbed and the rope was still dangling from the ceiling.

Slavish grabbed the rope and started to climb, a moment later he dropped back to the floor.

'I think I've discovered a flaw in our plan,' he said sheepishly.

'What?'

'Normally you would just give me a boost and I would help pull you up, but these ceilings are quite high.'

'What are you trying to say Murk?'

'I can't climb the rope.'

'Let me have a go, maybe I can help pull you up.'

Mug grabbed the rope.

'Must be the weight of the loot,' he said after several unsuccessful attempts.

'Yes that's it. Definitely,' Slavish agreed.

'Now what?'

'Front door?'

'Suppose so.' Together they traversed the long hallway towards the ballroom, their torchlight bouncing off several statues and paintings. They crossed the open expanse of the ballroom together, step-by-step and side-by-side, each taking turns to face the way they'd come from, *ninja style*. They made it through to the entry foyer which was dimly lit by a fire from the adjoining living room. In the flickering half-light, Mug could see a grey-haired man asleep in an armchair with a book in his lap. A Jack Russell was also nestled and asleep alongside him.

Mug pointed to his eyes and then to the dog. Slavish nodded. Very slowly and with deliberate steps they made their way to the front door. As Mug turned the handle, the latch made a noise. They both swung their heads around to look at the dog. Its ears had pricked up, but its eyes remained shut. They opened the heavy door and snuck outside. As they closed the door the bolt made a loud clack as it slotted into place. Mug and Slavish sprinted for the darkness as the dog leapt off Justine's Dad's lap and started barking like mad, their hearts racing. From within the shadows of the garden, Mug could hear Justine's Dad say, 'What is it boy? Is there something there?'

Yes, Mug silently answered. Mug could see a face look through the blinds by the front door. Mug held his breath.

'There's nothing there.' Justine's Dad said to the dog. Mug

breathed a sigh of relief. Slavish passed the bags over to Murky and then went and retrieved the rope, replaced the manhole cover and finally the tiles on the roof. A few moments later they had glided the ladder over to the street side of the fence and were on their way.

They drove a few blocks away and pulled over. In the back of the van they divided up the cash and put the contents of the second safe into a separate backpack. Mug said he'd go and see his fence, Connor, about the gold tomorrow.

'Would you guys like to come?'

'No, not really. I trust you,' said Murky, 'besides, Connor gives me the creeps, he's always on edge.'

'He's always dealing with criminals and doesn't know if one might double-cross him, give him a break,' Mug said.

'At least he has a soft spot for you,' said Slavish.

'That's because I've dealt with him for years and we don't waste each other's time...anyway I better get the contents of the second safe to Justine. I feel weird just having it on me.'

'Yeah fair enough.'

'What took you guys so long?' Murky asked.

Mug and Slavish looked at each other, 'the weight of the loot meant we couldn't leave the way we intended...' Slavish began in reply.

'Yeah, the weight was too much,' Mug confirmed, hoping the point wouldn't be questioned. Mug explained how the caper had nearly been undone by a dog which wasn't large enough to scare a rat.

Murky removed all the signs from the van, while Mug and Slavish changed their clothes. Murky drove them to their usual post-robbery spot to burn the clothes and scatter the ashes. Murky then drove them to Bacchus Bar.

Slavish ordered a round of drinks while Mug called Justine.

'Job's done,' he said without introducing himself.

'But they don't go away until next weekend!' Justine exclaimed.

'You said they were going away for the weekend on the twelfth.'

'No I said they were going away for a week on the twenty-first.'

Mug cringed. He was embarrassed by his dyslexia and the one time he tried to compensate for it, it wasn't needed.

'Anyway, it's done,' he replied.

'Now what?'

'Meet me at the bar.'

'When?'

'How about now?' Mug said.

'Fine. I'll be there as soon as I can,' Justine paused, '… tell me what it is.'

'Just come to the bar and you'll see.' Mug hung up and wondered how long it would take Justine to get there.

Twenty-nine minutes later, Justine walked into the bar. 'Justine Time,' Mug thought to himself mirthfully, 'another minute and I would've had to order another drink.' Murky and Slavish had left to celebrate the successful operation with their family and girlfriend respectively.

Justine sat down in the booth without making contact with the table.

'Please, may I have it?' she asked without any pleasantries.

Mug gave her the backpack. Justine unzipped it, peered inside and then raised an eyebrow. Just as Mug had when he'd seen it for the first time. She pulled out the object and began examining it. A few moments later she gasped.

'Will it meet your needs?' Mug asked curiously.

'Yes, I think it'll do nicely,' Justine replied with a relieved smile.

After a pause, she asked, 'did you have any trouble?'

Mug smiled. 'Maybe,' he replied, then seeing concern on Justine's face added, 'nothing to worry about, we just nearly got made by their dog.'

'Jacky is not a real dog. Shepherds and Labs are real dogs, that thing is an overgrown rat.'

'You're being a bit harsh.'

'Maybe, but even a decade ago when I was forty and they got him, I was happy they'd given him a silly name. My opinion hasn't changed since, despite my issues experiencing such things.'

'Now it can all be behind you.'

'Yes, I suppose so,' she sighed as though she was trying to let the weight lift off her shoulders.

'What are you going to do?'

'Confront them before they go away next week I suppose. I need to allow time for them to discover it has been taken. I take it you left enough evidence of your break in?'

Mug thought about the footprints on the bathroom wall from his now burnt boots; left as they'd attempted to climb back into the ceiling; the deliberately misplaced tiles on the roof; the painting concealing the first safe being left ajar and the mangled panel from the second safe.

'Yeah, yes we did. It'll look like a professional hit,' Mug said confidently.

'You'll mail me an appropriately sized package on Tuesday then — for appearances sake?'

'Yes,' Mug said.

'Good,' Justine replied in a manner sufficient to bring proceedings to a close. She took another look in the backpack, smiled and said 'I can't believe we're related to him. It would ruin my family if it got out.' She slung the backpack over her shoulder and walked out of the bar, looking taller than when she'd walked in. Mug watched her leave and took the last sip of his drink. He shook his head. It obviously meant something to Justine, but really, all of that for a family tree?

Acknowledgments

This collection came from wanting to find a home for some stories I'd written for *Movemind* which wound up not quite fitting (although Mug and his crew are in *The Lost Chapter* from that collection). I was going to include these stories in *Colours of Death*, but they were culled once again as they didn't fit the colour theme nor the more serious of the other stories. The working title of this collection was, therefore, 'Culled Capers,' but that changed when *The Coat Hanger* found a home in the anthology *The First Line* by the Monash Writers Group.

The idea to write some caper stories came from reading *Thieves Dozen* by Donald E. Westlake. I pay homage to this recognised Grand Master (Mystery Writers of America) in the first line of The Coat Hanger. I've also used the concept of having the thief steal an unusual object, which Westlake used frequently. I hope you've enjoyed reading this book. If you have, please leave a positive review on Amazon.com, Goodreads and social media.

About the Author

According to his wife, Robert has spent too much of his life studying. She has a point as he's earned seven tertiary qualifications. Robert has degrees in psychology, sociology, biology and education, all of which inspire his writing. He lives in Melbourne with his wife and two children. He likes writing stories which shift the perspective of the reader and make use of scientific concepts. Robert is mildly kosmemophobic.

When he was in high school, a dare escalated a little too quickly and Robert made the state final in an interpretive dance competition.

If you've enjoyed this book you may also like Robert New's other books, *Incite Insight, Movemind* and *Colours of Death.*

Incite Insight

While investigating why a victim's brain has melted, Detective Brad Thomas uncovers an intelligence raising program which he begins working through. As he makes progress, he finds his thinking being transformed. Brad uncovers the secretive Network of Freethinkers who are behind the program's development. He works his way through their initiation processes to become a member, but will he help them change the way the world is run?

The story has been described as "smart and imaginative" and "deceptively educational of the human condition."

Movemind: Speculative Short Stories

This twelve story collection is centred around the theme of being altered by a situation. In the acclaimed *How to Win a War,* a soldier experiences a strategy for ending wars which might just work. In *The Patriotic Amnesiac*, a mother voluntarily gives up her ability to form new memories with far-reaching consequences. A Queen and a Prime Minister plot against a President in *Sever-Reign. The Legend of Legend* is a light-hearted caper about an egg which contains a universal truth. In the dystopian *The Second Fear* a Ministry attempts to produce fear in someone who is literally fearless. In the closing story, *Devilish Tricks*, a deal with the Devil changes Casimir Hendrix's life, but is it for the better?

The collection has been praised by Sarah Stuart (author of the *Royal Command* series) for its "wicked twists" and "grippingly readable" stories.

Colours of Death: Sergeant Thomas' Casebook

From the author of *Movemind* and *Incite Insight*, comes a collection of nine detective stories where colour plays a role in the mystery.

Blue Bloods: A high school awards ceremony turns to tragedy when the audience turns blue as they die.

The 11th Killer: A serial killer's hair colour may be the key to their capture.

The Storyteller: An arsonist is killing people in house fires just so he can write a story about the rescuers.

Black Death: After a body is dumped in public, working out how the victim died is harder than decoding the intended message.

Fear the Red Man: An incident with the Red Man haunts Detective Thomas, but may also be the key to solving a new case.

Robert's book has been described as "intriguing and very insightful" and having "interesting and authentic twists."

www.ingramcontent.com/pod-product-compliance
Ingram Content Group UK Ltd.
Pitfield, Milton Keynes, MK11 3LW, UK
UKHW041849190726
13854UKWH00002B/788